中国南方著名古典史诗英译丛书

丛书主编　张立玉　起国庆

白族古典史诗

（汉英对照）

上

陆家瑞　乐夫　李俊祺　等　整理

皋峰　英译

［美］H.W. Lan　审校

出品单位：

中南民族大学南方少数民族文库翻译研究基地

WUHAN UNIVERSITY PRESS

武汉大学出版社

图书在版编目(CIP)数据

白族古典史诗. 上 = Classic Poetry of the Bai People(Volume 1):
英汉对照 / 陆家瑞等整理 ; 皋峰英译 . -- 武汉 : 武汉大学出版社,
2025.8. -- 中国南方著名古典史诗英译丛书 / 张立玉,起国庆主编 .
ISBN 978-7-307-25053-6

Ⅰ. I222.7

中国国家版本馆 CIP 数据核字第 2025Q7J871 号

责任编辑:李晶晶　　　责任校对:鄢春梅　　　版式设计:韩闻锦

出版发行:**武汉大学出版社**　(430072　武昌　珞珈山)

(电子邮箱:cbs22@whu.edu.cn　网址:www.wdp.com.cn)

印刷:武汉邮科印务有限公司

开本:720×1000　1/16　印张:9.75　字数:111 千字　插页:1

版次:2025 年 8 月第 1 版　2025 年 8 月第 1 次印刷

ISBN 978-7-307-25053-6　定价:68.00 元

丛书编委会

序

在千古悠悠的历史长河中，中华民族以自己的勤劳和智慧创造了光辉灿烂的古典史诗。古典史诗是一种结构庞大、富有综合性特征的民间长篇叙事诗，一般分为创世史诗、英雄史诗和迁徙史诗三大类，其内容丰富、气势恢弘，在漫长的传承过程中，融进了大量的民间神话、传说、故事、歌谣和谚语等，是一个民族社会生产活动、宗教信仰、风俗习惯和历史文化知识的一种特殊总汇。它经过长期的积累，深深积淀于中华民族的精神文化宝库之中，是千百年来中华民族自尊、自信、自爱、自强意识的重要源泉。它对中华民族文化传统的形成和发展产生了巨大而深远的影响。

近年来，为了推动中华文化的国际传播、提升中华文化的影响力、深入挖掘中华文化的精神内核、让中国优秀传统文化走出去，中南民族大学南方少数民族文库翻译研究基地积极对中国南方非遗文化典籍进行对外传播和译介的工作。该基地民族典籍英译捷报频传、硕果累累。先后出版了土家族典籍英译2部，纳西族三大史诗英译3部，“十三五”国家重点图书、国家出版基金项目“中国南方民间文学典籍英译丛书”14部。

近日，该翻译研究基地又传来佳音：他们要出版“中国南方著名古典史诗英译丛书”。这套丛书包括十余本，分别是《苗族古歌》《巴塔麻嘎捧尚罗》《厘俸》《阿昌族、德昂族古典史诗》《阿黑西尼摩》《相勐》《阿细的先基》《白族古典史诗（上、下）》《拉祜族创世史诗》《傈僳族叙事诗》《德傣掸登俄》。这些典籍多数入围了国家级非物质文化遗产名录，展示了不同民族的文化。

《苗族古歌》又称“大歌”，作为苗族的创世史诗，它是苗族口传文学的典型代表，也是记录苗族古代社会的一部百科全书。它于2006年5月20日被国务院批准列入第一批国家级非物质文化遗产名录。苗族的各种文化艺术都可以从这里找到它们的源头，《苗族古歌》的内容森罗万象，有苗族的发展史、远古时期的开天辟地、繁衍人类、耕耘劳作、衣食住行、婚丧嫁娶、重建家园，还有苗族人民长期遭受压迫和剥削而反抗以争取自由幸福的生活等内容。它不仅具有历史学、民族学、哲学、人类学的研究价值，还具有教育、审美和娱乐等方面的杰出价值；它是研究远古思想的形象化材料，是苗族历史的艺术写照，也是了解苗族社会习俗的窗口。

《巴塔麻嘎捧尚罗》为傣族创世史诗，是傣族文学的巅峰之作，也是我国南方少数民族创世史诗的经典之作。与《乌沙巴罗》《粘芭西顿》《兰嘎西贺》《粘响》一同被傣族人民称作“五大诗王”。《巴塔麻嘎捧尚罗》融合了傣族本土的神话叙事与外来的佛经叙事，经过历代歌手的不断演述以及文人创编成文、誊抄成本，逐渐实现书面化和系统化，最终形成了15000多行的长篇史诗。这部史诗内容宏大，包括天神英叭诞生、英叭开天辟地、众神诞生、地球毁灭又重生、布桑嘎西与雅桑嘎赛修补天地又捏土造人、葫芦孕育万物、天神制定历法、桑木底教人造屋定居、人类大兴旺、民族迁徙等内容。

《厘俸》是一部在傣族文学史上具有重大意义的英雄史诗，主要叙述了古代英雄海罕和俸改之间的战争，并展示了傣族先民从原始社会解体到奴隶制初期广阔的社会生活。《厘俸》是傣族文学史乃至文化史上一部具有里程碑意义的作品，是傣族形成和崛起期所有重大历史事件、军事行动、社会生活、时代风尚、英雄崇拜、信仰体系以及各种英雄传说的历史积淀和艺术创造的结晶。它具有民族史、民族学、宗教学、文化学、文艺学等多学科的价值，堪称傣族古代社会文化的“百科全书”，是一部不可多得的文化遗产。

《阿昌族、德昂族古典史诗》由阿昌族和德昂族两个民族的史诗组成。阿昌族古典史诗《遮帕麻和遮米麻》是流传于云南省德宏傣族景颇族自治州梁河县的传统民间文学，2006 年 5 月被列入第一批国家级非物质文化遗产名录。《遮帕麻和遮米麻》产生于阿昌族早期，是一部讲述阿昌族先民为了感谢遮帕麻和遮米麻的创世之恩，以及补天缝地、降魔降妖等多次挽救人类的大恩大德的民间文学作品，涵括了创世神话、人类起源神话、洪水神话，也包含了人祖英雄神话。这部长诗同时也形象地反映了人类从母权制向父权制过渡的状况。德昂族古典史诗《达古达楞格莱标》是流传于云南省德宏傣族景颇族自治州的民间文学，2008 年被列入第二批国家级非物质文化遗产名录，也是德昂族迄今发掘、整理并出版的唯一一部创世史诗。与其他民族的创世史诗不同，《达古达楞格莱标》情节单纯，始终以万物之源——茶为主线，集中地描写了这一人类和大地上万物的始祖如何化育世界、繁衍人类的神迹，并以奇妙的幻想将茶拟人化，提出人类来源于茶树、德昂族是茶树的子孙的独特观点。

《阿黑西尼摩》是彝族创世史诗，流传于云南省元阳县彝族地区。中文版由施文科、李亮文唱述，罗希吾戈、普学旺翻译，收入《云南少数民族古典史诗全集(上卷)》，并入选“中华大国学经典文库”。全诗由序歌、阿黑西尼摩生万物、人类的起源、天地开始分、叭依定历法、旱灾、洪水泛滥、天地生日、长寿和死亡、婚嫁的起源和演变、祭祀兴起等部分组成，是彝族典籍文化的重要组成部分，具有重要的文化价值和历史价值。该史诗中的“神谱”自成系统，内容丰富，幻想奇特，在阐释天地万物的起源方面独树一帜，对研究彝族原始文化，特别是母体崇拜以及人类母系文化，均具有重要价值。

《相勐》取材于傣族历史上部落战争的重大事件，真实地反映了傣族古代社会由部落林立到部落联盟直至最后形成统一的历史进程，展示了广阔的社会生活，塑造了各种英雄人物，显示了民族崛起期——英雄时代的民族精神。在艺术手法上，作品采用框架叙事结构，即以一个故事贯穿全诗，再以大故事套小故事，使情节的发展变化纷繁又紧扣中心。此外，作品语言清新、优美，充分体现出傣族传统诗歌的独特韵味。《相勐》以其特定的历史价值与艺术成就，被称为傣族最为成熟的一部英雄史诗。

《阿细的先基》是彝族支系阿细人的史诗、彝族四大创世史诗之一，由云南弥勒县西山一带的阿细人民口头流传，以固定的“先基调”演唱而得名。在表现形式上采用“先基调”进行演唱，往往通过对唱提问、对答的方式展开诗篇。句式一般为五言，但到了“求爱”等感情激烈的段落时，间用六言和长短句，以便于抒情。全诗分两部分。第一部分“最古的时候”叙述天地万物的起源和人类早期的生活习俗。第二部分“男女说合成一家”记叙阿细人独特的婚姻和风俗习惯。具有传承意义。

拉祜族创世史诗《牡帕密帕》是拉祜族宗教文化的核心部分之一。拉祜族以“卑咯斯”(Birec)为神，他被认为是宇宙的创造者。《牡帕密帕》记录了对卑咯斯的崇拜方式、神话故事以及人们对神灵的祭祀活动。在拉祜族的历史中，这部史诗被传唱和演绎了几百年，并以其独特的形式和内涵成为了拉祜族宗教文化的重要组成部分，被视为拉祜族文化的瑰宝，它记录了拉祜族的起源、神话传说、社会生活等内容。这一史诗的传承与发展是拉祜族文化传承与发展的缩影。

其余几本书展示了白族、傈僳族等的风俗习惯、恋爱故事、斗争故事等。《白族古典史诗(上、下)》中的《串权连》《青姑娘》《鸿雁传书》三部长诗是白族文化典籍。《串权连》热情歌颂了一对白族青年的自由恋爱和他们的坚贞爱情，突出表现了白族人民对“指腹为婚”这一残酷的封建婚姻制度的反抗。《青姑娘》则通过反映旧社会一个童养媳的不幸遭遇，揭露和控诉了封建礼教对青年妇女的残酷迫害。《鸿雁传书》描写的是一对青年夫妻，丈夫出门谋生，远离家乡，二人分居两地，他们只有托鸿雁传书，互相倾诉思念之情。《白族古典史诗(上、下)》中的《出门调》主要流传在云南剑川、洱源、兰坪等县和丽江、九河等白族地区，这部叙述诗通篇用第一人称演唱。它集中描写了剑川木匠出门在外的悲苦生活。而《出门恋歌》虽然也描写了男主人公因生活所迫，不得已与心爱的人分离、外出讨生活的情节，但重点讲述男女主人公从相知相恋到分离后相思成疾，最终欢喜重逢的故事。

《傈僳族叙事诗》中的《生产调》生动形象地反映了傈僳族人民的日常生产劳动，表现了他们勤劳、善良、友爱、互助的民族性格和美好的民族风尚。《盖房调》为傈僳族古老的传统调子，来源于傈僳族盖房子的劳动。它对傈僳族古老的盖房习俗、住房结构、盖房时的劳动场面均作了真实、细致的描绘，这对人们研究傈僳族的社会生活具有重要的参考价值。《种瓜调》流传于怒江傈僳族自治州的碧江、泸水、福贡、贡山等地的傈僳族人民中，是傈僳族口头诗歌中流传比较广、影响较深的作品，诗中所说的南瓜发芽、出苗、串藤、开花、结瓜，实际上指的是男女青年爱情的成长过程。

《德傣掸登俄》是壮族土僚支系中广为流传的一部创世史诗，由开天辟地、洪水淹天、土僚创世、星女下凡四个部分组成。第一部分的内容为：天地是罗扎、罗妞开辟出来的，万物是罗扎、罗妞制造成的；第二部分的内容为：洪水淹天之后，在葫芦里躲过劫难的两兄妹结为夫妻，传下了人种；第三部分的内容为：土僚先民种稻种棉，铸造铁器，创造了美好生活；第四部分的内容为：天上的星女下凡与罗傣结婚，犹如爱神，为此，每年三月初三，土僚都要祭祀星女。整部长诗共两千多行，绝大部分为五言体，叙事奇特、结构紧密、内容丰富、韵味十足，经常由长老在举办红、白喜事时或节日期间吟诵，颇受群众欢迎。现仍广泛流传于红河流域的壮族地区。

这些故事都很引人入胜，都很符合国家文化发展需求，向世人讲述中国故事、传播中华文化，并且讲述的是中国少数民族故事，充分体现了党和国家对各民族的关怀。这些典籍中折射出的文化多样性极大地丰富了世界文化，使世界文化更加丰富多彩、绚丽多姿。因此，民族典籍英译是传播中国文化、文学和文明的重要途径，是中华文化走出去的重要组成部分，是提高文化软实力的重要方式，在文化交流和文明建设中起着不可或缺的作用，对提高中国对外话语权和构建中国对外话语体系、对建设世界文学都有积极意义。

张立玉　起国庆

2023年12月

前 言

《白族古典史诗》上册主要由《出门调》《出门恋歌》《巧木匠》组成。《出门调》主要流传在剑川、洱源、兰坪等县和丽江、九河等白族地区。这部长诗叙述了一个木匠出门谋生的悲惨生活经历。为了养家糊口，木匠辞别妻子外出帮工，本打算挣点零钱第二年就回家春耕，岂知在王都司(旧时县级负责地方治安的武官)家干了一年，王都司不但不给工钱，反诬蔑他偷窃金手圈，木匠告到官府，因为官官相护，他反被判给王家抵作家奴。服役七八年，他满腹冤情无处诉，后得以逃脱，在山神(木匠中的为首者)的帮助下找到活计。他外出十年，始得返乡和家人、妻子团聚。这部作品在民间流传中多有异文，尽管情节异同不一，但在揭露旧社会的黑暗及表现劳动人民家庭中夫妻间的深情厚爱方面，却是所有文本所共有的。

《出门恋歌》是典型的白族“本子曲”，它由“初见”“定情”“起誓”“别离”“相思”“疑云”和“重逢”等几个章节组成。故事情节与流传于剑川、洱源、兰坪等县的《出门调》有许多相似之处，但《出门调》集中描写的是剑川木匠出门在外的悲苦生活，而《出门恋歌》虽然也描写了男主人公因生活所迫不得不与心爱的人儿分离、外出讨生活的情节，但重点还是在讲述男女主人公从相知相恋到分离后相思成疾，最终欢喜重逢的恋情。与众多的白族爱情长诗相比，这是一篇带有明显喜剧色彩的爱情长诗。

《巧木匠》也是白族的一首传统歌曲，讲述了一个聪明的木匠如何通过他的智慧和技巧，制作出完美的三弦，吸引了金翅鸟变成名叫梨花的姑娘与之成家。梨花姑娘后又被坏人张有财抢婚，跳入漾江。每年七月七，梨花与巧木匠变成彩霞在空中相会。这首歌展示了白族人民对智慧和技艺的高度尊重，同时也体现了他们对爱情和幸福的深深向往。

白族民歌内容丰富、题材广泛、生动活泼，历史故事、社会生活、劳动生产、山川景物、爱情婚姻等都融于歌词之中。它们节奏自由，曲调悠扬，纯朴自然，人们常在山野间吟唱。在文学价值方面，白族民歌也是中国民间文学的瑰宝。

目 录

Contents

出　门　调

手持三弦弹不响，
未成曲调泪千行；
悲歌一曲《出门调》，
句句痛肝肠。

一、商量出门

秋风吹来秋草黄，
大雁南飞一行行；
四方匠艺相邀约，
出门走忙忙。

叫声贤妻娃娃嫫，
叫声贤妻娃娃娘；
心头有着一件事，
想和你商量。

田租地租利息重，
一年到头空奔忙；
辛苦一年无所得，
家无隔夜粮。

Seeking a Livelihood Elsewhere

Three-string-instrument in hand,
And tears in my eyes,
I play the tune of *Seeking a Livelihood Elsewhere*,
Every note of which makes me feel sad.

I. Negotiation of Leaving Home

The autumn wind turns grass yellow,
While geese fly south in rows;
Craftsmen from all directions gather,
Intending to go out for bread.

My virtuous wife,
My beloved wife,
There is something in my mind
That I want to discuss with you.

We have rents and interests yet to pay,
Even though we work in every possible way,
After one year of hard work,
Still no food for the coming day.

我想收拾出门去，
趁着冬闲下迤南；
挣它几文血汗钱，
救救急和难。

丈夫打算出远门，
叫我两眼泪淋淋；
爹嫫年老娃娃小，
咋个去得成？

家中没有当家汉，
应门应户也无人；
出伕出役哪个去？
哪个去应名？

搭伙吃的多依果，
搭伙念本苦经文；
千斤重担搭伙挑，
不让你出门。

叫声贤妻仔细听，
就为担子重千斤；
今年秋谷收回来，
佃主要平分。

冬至节交米租子，
债息债利难付清，
麻索草鞋通了底，
剩下四条筋。

I'd pack up and go out there,
Going south in the slack season of winter;
A few pennies with hard work
Shall cater for urgent need.

You plan to go for a long journey,
Leaving me behind in tears;
Parents are old and children young,
How can I make it?

Without a man in the house,
Who is to answer the door and take care of things?
Who will go out to work?
Who will take on the responsibility?

We eat together,
And recite scriptures together;
So we'd shoulder the responsibility together,
And I won't let you go out.

My virtuous wife,
Even if we sow much,
Upon autumn harvest,
The landlord shall demand a fair share.

We'd pay rice and rent on winter solstice,
And also debts and interests;
The grass shoes were worn out,
No more days to wear.

剩下秕谷两三斗，
老小怎么度光阴？
莫奈何才下潞江，
去苦拼苦拼。

我知丈夫你心肠，
也知出门谋生难；
腹中愁肠十八拐，
心里乱如麻。

人说潞江瘴气重，
阴雨蒙蒙起痼霞；
五黄六月发摆子，
提起心发慌。

再说世道不清平，
兵匪盗贼难提防；
我劝丈夫莫去了，
搭伙度饥寒。

为躲饥寒度时光，
我才狠心走夷方；
赡老养小当家汉，
顶雪又踩霜。

爹嫫脚上没双鞋，
妻子身上没衣裳；
小女小儿这两个，
饿得把口张。

With few leftovers,
How can we survive?
No choice left but go to to Lujiang,
To struggle and work hard.

My dear husband,
I know seeking a livelihood elsewhere is hard;
I am just worried,
And my mind is in chaos.

They say Lujiang has heavy miasma,
Misty rain brings up chronic sores;
In May and June, when it is easy to catch malaria,
I start to panic.

Also the world is unpeaceful,
And bandits and thieves lurk;
I'd advise my beloved not to go,
Let's face difficulties together.

To avoid hunger and cold and pass the hard times,
I have to go to farthest places with a hard heart;
Supporting the old and raising the young as a man of the house,
Braving snow and trampling frost.

My parents have no shoes on their feet.
My wife has no clothes on her body;
My little danghter and son,
Hungry with their mouths open.

我有手艺在身上，
房子盖过几十枋；
一高两低双楼廓，
尺寸心中装。

方五斜七九五墨，
见尺收分不会差；
上七下八五分水，
美观又大方。

装修隔整拿手活，
会刨会凿会雕花；
红漆黑漆罩金漆，
样样是行家。

粗活细活盘不倒，
会做像眼梅花窗；
妻你放我下迤南，
挣几文钱花。

一根苦藤把心牵，
苦心空悬腹中间；
丽江粑粑两面烤，
两面受熬煎。

不让你去又不成，
让你去了又心酸；
左右为难无主意，
心辣如醋腌。

Skills have I mastered,
And dozens of houses built;
For double-storeyed buildings with different heights,
I'd measure and design in my mind.

Square five, diagonal seven, and nine-five marking,
I will not miss one millimeter on the ruler;
Seven top, eight bottom, and five to half,
The pattern shall be beautiful and generous.

Skilled in interior decoration and partitioning,
I can plane, chisel, and carve flowers;
Making red lacquer, black lacquer, or lacquer covered with gold,
I am an expert at everything.

Be it rough and delicate tasks,
Or window with plum blossom patterns;
My dear wife, let me go,
I'd make some money to spend.

Sadness and worry
In my mind,
As Lijiang pancakes grilled on both sides,
I was tormented both inside and out.

It won't work if I insist,
Yet it breaks my heart letting you go;
I was caught in a dilemma,
Bitter as hell.

左也难来右也难，
好似跌落在深渊；
思前想后心不定，
用啥做盘缠？

提起盘缠心发慌，
话到口边暗心伤；
家中小猪这一对，
忍心卖掉它。

土布买它小半件，
补补儿女破衣裳；
爹嫫年老畏风寒，
鞋子买两双。

剩下几文做盘缠，
麻布毯子买一张；
穷人日子真难过，
医医眼前疮。

听得卖猪暗心伤，
好似六月降寒霜；
背时主意你莫打，
莫出馊主张。

家中小猪这一对，
全家生活指望它；
等到明春猪长大，
换粮度春荒。

To go or not to go,
I feel lost;
And cannot make up my mind.
What about the travelling expenses?

I'd panic speaking of travelling expenses,
Feel sad and utter no words.
I have no choice but sell
The two little pigs at home.

I'd buy some cloth,
And make some clothes for the kids,
And two pairs of shoes,
For our aging parents.

Sparing some for travelling expenses,
I'd also buy a hemp blanket;
Life is really difficult for the poor,
With wounds yet to heal.

Great sorrow when hearing about selling the pigs,
It feels like a cold frost in June;
Don't ever think about the pigs again,
That's just a foolish idea.

The pair of little pigs,
We depend on them for a living;
The pigs shall grow up soon
And we'd exchange for food in spring famine.

叫声贤妻莫高声，
爹嫫听着会伤心；
只为家境多困苦，
才下这狠心。

你我夫妻十多年，
黄连伴着黄柏生；
黄连伴着黄柏长，
苦根连苦根。

豌豆开花角对角，
麻打草鞋筋连筋；
草鞋泡着黄连水，
从头苦到根。

家务好比千斤担，
千斤重担不算轻；
牛轭横架脖子上，
奔不起也奔。

一对小猪怀中抱，
忍心去把猪卖掉；
猪钱刚刚拿到手，
乡约就来到。

红嘴白牙淌口水，
两只眼睛如鹰鹞；
催捐逼款要银钱，
拦路的强盗。

My dear wife, lower your voice.
Mom and dad will be sad to hear us.
It's only because of family hardship
That I made this tough decision.

Married for over ten years,
Life is hard,
And harder for
The two of us.

Peas bloom in pairs,
Grass shoes soak
And break easily.
It's bitterness all over.

Household chores
Are never easy.
With a yoke on the neck,
A cow is to plough.

Holding pigs in my arms,
I go to the market for sale;
Money in my hand,
Yet villains soon blocked my way.

They wear evil looks,
And their eyes vicious.
They demanded nothing but money.
Real rascals on the road.

岭上獐精山中虎，
敲骨吸髓如虎豹；
盘缠实在难凑足，
向谁去贷告？

盘缠实在凑不够，
典桑卖田把银凑；
三分田典一两银，
受不起也受。

生漆赊它一小桶，
吃升回斗利息重；
利息再重也得赊，
大泻吃巴豆。

市上漆价七八分，
余价一钱五左右；
重利盘剥生意客，
设下杀人扣。

心忧忧，
生吞杨梅酸溜溜；
心中好似毛虫爬，
时时把心揪。

无心料理针线活，
浑身上下冷飕飕；
六神无主心不定，
忧心实难收。

They lurk in the mountains like tigers.
There's never enough for them.
Without enough traveling expenses,
Who can I borrow from?

Still not enough traveling expenses,
I'd pawn the mulberry field and sell the land;
More field pawned for little money,
That's just the cost we have to bear.

I'd buy some lacquer on credit,
And the interest is high.
I have no choice
But drink poison in time of thirst.

The lacquer costs only a few on the market
Yet fifteen on credit.
With also high interests,
It's just a trap for customers.

I am deeply sad and worried.
It feels like a caterpillar
Crawling in my heart,
Making me rattled.

I am not in the mood for needlework,
And feel cold all over my body;
I just can't settle down,
And anxiety dominates.

我劝贤妻莫忧伤，
男儿有志走四方；
出门不止我一个，
你莫心怏怏。

旧衣几件补一补，
草鞋打它一两双；
邻舍借升荞麦面，
烤几个粑粑。

观音寺里许个愿，
本主庙里烧炷香；
祈求神灵保吉利，
一路保平安。

二、依依惜别

白悠悠，
小小弯月照九州；
送夫出门到村口，
清风冷飕飕。

天边寒星伴月走，
月如弯钩把心揪；
今朝别离何日见，
离愁何日休？

弯弯残月往西偏，
冷冷寒光照平川，

My dear, don't worry,
A man shall have ambitions.
And I'm not out there all alone,
Please rest assured.

I'd repair the old clothes,
Make a couple of grass shoes;
Borrow some flour from neighbors,
And bake you some bread.

I'd also go to the Guanyin Temple,
Burn incense at the main temple;
Pray to the gods for good luck,
And to protect you all the way.

II. Farewell

White as a plate,
The moon shines on the ground.
I see off my husband at the village entrance,
Cold wind blowing on my face.

Cold stars go with the crescent moon
Which hooks my heart.
When will we meet again
And my sorrow end?

The moon turns west a bit,
While moonlight casts on the ground.

贤妻送我出远门，
送到大路边。

大路茫茫无尽头，
寒山点点绕青烟；
青烟也知别离苦，
缕缕挂山巅。

月落星沉黑茫茫，
送夫出门过荷塘；
塘中藕断丝不断，
丝丝扯肝肠。

此去他乡如孤雁，
独自投宿独飞翔；
莫为银钱恋他乡，
莫把老小忘。

贤妻送我到桥头，
罗城桥上几回首，
眼泪打落桥面上，
泪如江水流。

江水悠悠流不断，
流到天涯海尽头；
离妻别子走他乡，
无限别离愁。

My dear wife sees me off
By the great road.

The road ahead is vast with no end,
While mist hovers around cold mountains.
The mist must have known the bitterness of farewell,
Why else would it stay so high on the top?

It turns all black without moon and stars,
I see off my husband, passing by the lotus pond.
The lotus stays connected even when separated,
As we shall be.

Away from home you'd be all alone,
And rely all on yourself.
Don't ever forget home for money.
Don't ever forget family.

Dear wife bids farewell on the bridge,
And looks back many times.
Tears drop on the bridge,
As water flowing in the river.

Water in the river flows forever,
To the depths of the ocean.
Saying goodbye to my family,
Leaving behind endless homesickness.

江水悠悠往南流，
手攀柳树折枝柳；
柳枝插在河岸上，
取名望夫柳。

大雁不过三月三，
小燕不过九月九；
来年春暖柳发芽，
你要转回头。

望夫柳下情依依，
叫声别了把泪挥；
长空寒雁也成对，
我自独自飞。

贤妻在家多保重，
人心不测是与非；
世道炎凉人情薄，
莫早出晚归。

阿爹阿嫫托给你，
莫使他们常伤悲；
小儿小女在身边，
早晚需依偎。

莫忙走，
扭丝银镯脱下手；
银镯放进兜肚里，
藏在你胸口。

The river stretches southwards,
While I pick a willow branch.
Stick it by the bank,
And name it Husband-Awaiting Willow.

The wild geese migrate back in March,
And the sparrows in September.
When the willow tree buds next year,
You'd come back to me.

Farewell under the willow tree,
Tears filled my eyes.
The wild geese fly in pairs,
Yet I am now all alone.

My dear wife, take care.
Human hearts are hard to get,
And the world is fickle.
Don't go out too early or home late.

They are all on you, Mom and Dad,
Don't let them be sad.
Our boy and girl, keep by your side,
And be with them at dawn and night.

Wait a bit,
I have here my hair and bracelet.
Keep them in your pocket
And me in your chest.

天边寒雁各自飞，
打齐筷子各一头；
手镯拴住两颗心，
银丝绺扣绺。

银镯头，
银丝股股绺扣绺；
贤妻放心转回去，
深情记心头。

天上三星来作证，
真情一片对北斗；
只为家穷暂分离，
回来共白头。

翠莹莹，
何必发誓请三星；
夫妻风雨十多年，
知你最坚贞。

此去冷暖自料理，
缝补浆洗自操心；
家中虽然多困苦，
做活莫贪心。

千金万两总不够，
难填苦井万丈深；
挣得几文就回来，
宽慰父母心。

The wild geese fly on their own,
And the chopsticks only work when separated.
The bracelet shall have us connected,
And the hair locked.

With the silver bracelet
And the gray hair in hand,
Rest assured, my dear,
I'd love you forever.

Witnessed by the stars,
Love for you shall last.
Separated only for livelihood,
We'd be together when I come back.

Oh, my dear.
We don't need an oath.
We have been together for a decade,
I know you are faithful.

You are all alone out there,
And everything shall be on your own.
Even though life isn't easy,
Don't be too hard on yourself.

Money will never be enough,
And hardship is yet to be conquered.
Make some money and return soon,
Parents shall otherwise worry.

翠莹莹，
贤妻叮嘱记在心，
金玉良言嘱咐我，
点点记在心。

明春他乡布谷叫，
明年此地柳发青；
有钱无钱也回来，
从此不离分。

三、南行路上

出门谋生走夷方，
抛妻别子离家乡；
离乡背井别父母，
扯疼心和肝。

双脚好像千斤重，
山神坡上回头看；
回头遥见家乡面，
两眼泪汪汪。

砖头盖面石头城，
剑川古城四方方；
剑阳湖像一面镜，
粼粼闪金光。

金华山峰高入云，
墨斗山在坝中央；

Oh, my dear!
I'd keep every word you said,
Every piece of advice
And your love forever in mind.

When the cuckoo cries
And the willow buds next spring,
I'd be back with or without money,
And be with you forever.

III. On the Way South

Seeking a livelihood elsewhere,
Leaving behind my wife and children,
My father and mother,
Which makes me heartbroken.

My feet weigh me down,
And I stand on the hill and look back;
Bid farewell to my home again,
Tears filling my eyes.

Stone houses with tile roofs,
The ancient city of Jianchuan is square;
And the Jianyang Lake resembles a mirror,
Golden ripples waving above the lake.

Jinhua Peak towers into the clouds,
While Modou Mountain stands in the middle of the dam;

古道垂柳通长街，
通连十八乡。

十八乡村无闲人，
青壮纷纷走夷方；
田中耕作老和弱，
胡子白花花。

含悲忍泪往前走，
抬头看见回乡河；
回乡河水有乡情，
倒往剑川流。

伸手掬杯家乡水，
清清河水凉透喉；
喝下这口家乡水，
点滴在心头。

臭水井边走朝南，
一队官兵如虎狼；
这家进来那家出，
催银又催粮。

撵得鸡狗咽咽叫，
手中铁链叮当响；
巷口吆喝两三声，
赛过活阎王。

Willow trees grow by the long street
That connects all neighboring towns.

Young people from those towns
Have all gone out seeking a livelihood,
Leaving behind the elderly
And the weak in the field.

I trudge ahead,
Only to see the river alone.
Water in the river is so kind,
Flowing backwards home.

I scoop and drink some river water,
It is sweet and cool.
I'd forever remember
The taste of water home.

Step further south by the smelly well,
To see officers and soldiers robbing like hell,
House in and house out,
Taking money and grain.

Chicken and dogs flee about
Along with the shackle sound,
Shouting desperately in the alleys,
They are the living devils.

老人吓得腿打颤，
娃娃吓得哭爹娘；
穷人光景一个样，
心中好凄凉。

荷担束装往南行，
第一那晚宿三营；
他乡明月三更夜，
缕缕别离情。

我欲化作清风去，
明月清风归故境；
剑阳湖上转三转，
转回我门庭。

瞧见爹嫫倚门望，
瞧见我妻泪淋淋；
小儿牵衣把我叫，
也知别离情。

传来燋楼五更鼓，
一夜乡心到天明；
金鸡打鸣催行人，
忧忧登路程。

日暮黄昏鸟投林，
第二那晚宿沙坪；
风尘仆仆贪赶路，
一路冒风尘。

The elderly tremble
And the children cry,
Fate for the poor is similar.
It is just so sad.

I pack up and go further south.
On the first night I shift base three times.
The midnight moonlight here
Makes me homesick.

I'd like to be the wind,
Blowing along with the moon,
Spinning above Jianyang Lake,
And be back home.

I see mom and dad leaning by the gate,
My wife weeping bitterly;
Children cry out my name,
And I feel so homesick.

The midnight drum is knocked five times,
And I feel sad all night long.
The rooster crows,
While I start my journey heavy-hardheartedly.

The sun sets and birds nestle in the woods.
On the second night I lodge in Shaping.
I rush along the road,
Despite the fatigue.

老板点头迎宿客，
老板娘子来开门；
见我是个穷木匠，
脸上无表情。

柴火只给一小束，
豆大油灯黑沉沉；
有心想把灯芯挑，
又怕店主人。

人情势利处处有，
人越有钱心越狠；
古说："在家千日好，
穷汉莫出门。"

丢下饭碗出厨房，
只见店家乐洋洋；
你逗我爱天伦乐，
我心独自寒。

我爹我嫫受冻饿，
我儿我女挨饥寒；
我妻破衣不蔽体，
小脸蜡样黄。

爹嫫子女相分离，
哪天才能乐一堂？
想想世间不平事，
气烂我肝肠。

The boss nods to welcome an overnight guest,
And his wife opens the door;
Seeing that I am just a poor carpenter,
Her face is expressionless.

Given only a little bunch of firewood,
The oil lamp is dim.
I itch to trim the wick—
But the innkeeper is watching.

Humans are only selfish and worldly,
Even so are the rich people.
As the saying goes, "Home is the best,
And the poor shall be home."

Dropping off the bowl, stepping out of the kitchen,
I see only happiness on the shopkeeper's face.
They are having great fun,
While I sit sad and alone.

My parents are suffering.
My children are hungry.
My wife is dressed in rags,
And her face is pale.

My family is now separated,
When will we meet up?
Thinking of all the unfairness,
I feel sorrowful and angry.

沙坪往南海风紧，
二更才到大理城；
遇着提台捉木匠，
要盖望海亭。

木匠家什抢了去，
包袱抢得无踪影；
提台的兵那伙，
比贼还要狠。

日落星稀夜茫茫，
连夜逃到观音塘；
菩萨睁眼和尚睡，
门外把身藏。

只身只剩破墨斗，
孤孤此身实凄惶；
冷风凄凄腹中饥，
饥寒知夜长。

屋漏偏逢连夜雨，
小苗出土遭霜打；
进退两难无主意，
伤心泪千行。

孑然一身到蒙化，
大仓街上抬头望；
此地风光又不同，
有回又有汉。

The sea wind is strong further south of Shaping,
And I'd arrive at Dali around midnight.
I see the prefect capturing carpenters,
To build the Ocean-Observing Pavilion.

The carpenter's tools are robbed,
And luggage impounded.
Those soldiers are
Crueler than the thieves.

The sun sets and the stars come out.
I'd flee to Guanyin Pond overnight.
The monks have fallen asleep,
While I hide out behind the gate.

I have by my side
Only the marker,
Feeling cold and hungry
All the night.

The roof leaks on rainy night,
And seedlings suffer the frost often.
I am in a dilemma,
And tears blur my sight.

I arrive at Menghua all alone,
Standing on the street to observe.
The view here is quite different;
There are Hui and Han people.

彝家汉子黑包头，
花麻口袋横身挂；
回族妇女多缠足，
头顶花花帕。

大仓街上多商客，
喝酒猜拳把令唱；
踟蹰街头无人怜，
无钱买碗饭。

手中银钱无半文，
只有银镯在身上；
伸手兜肚掏手镯，
不忍低头看。

扭丝银镯丝扭丝，
此时苦楚有谁知！
徘徊街头心不定，
寒泪落满腮。

我妻本是贫家女，
心爱首饰这一只；
忍痛割爱交给我，
缕缕寄相思。

忍心兑得三吊钱，
铁匠铺里置家什；
小小偏斧打一把，
大小凿几只。

Young men of Yi wear black headcloth,
And clothes with flower-decorated pockets.
Women of Hui have small feet,
And wear a gorgeous scarf.

There are many merchants on the street of Dacang,
And many are drinking and playing finger-games.
Wandering on the street helplessly,
I have no money for food.

I have no money on my person,
But the silver bracelet.
I fish it out of the pocket,
And dare not look at it.

Silver bracelet in hand,
Who's to know my distress?
Wandering on the street,
I can't help tearing.

My dear wife is from a poor family,
And has nothing but this bracelet
That she gave to me
Out of complete love.

I exchange the bracelet for money
And buy some tools at the smithy:
A shiny axe,
And some chisels.

巍宝山高峰连峰，
峰峰高耸入云中；
天亮爬到朝天门，
日出红彤彤。

一步一拐太子殿，
玉皇阁转三清殿；
四脚四手往上爬，
两耳响嗡嗡。

长春洞下住一夜，
举目无亲此山中；
铺草垫叶盖衣服，
饥寒腹中空。

山风呼呼寒透骨，
睁着眼睛望星空；
弯卷胳臂当枕头，
一夜把火烘。

四、王家遭陷

景东境，
景东山谷接石层；
白云上面盖黑云，
霜雪满山顶。

秋风阵阵吹枯草，
兵荒马乱不太平；

Peaks of Weibao Mountain
Tower into the clouds.
I ascend to Chaotian Gate upon daybreak,
To see the rising sun red.

I make my way to Taizi Hall,
Yuhuang Pavilion and Sanqing Hall,
And climb upwards with all my strength,
With buzzing sound in my ears.

I stay under the Changchun Cave at night,
And no one in the mountain knows me.
Clothes as quilt, I sleep on grass and leaves.
Hunger and cold soon hit me hard.

Biting wind blowing by,
I stay up watching the starry sky,
Arm as pillow,
And bonfire by the side.

IV. Entrapped by the Wang Family

In the territory of Jingdong,
Jingdong peaks pile stone on stone.
Black cloud covers the white.
Frost and snow seal the summits.

Autumn wind withers the grass,
And the soldiers bring no peace.

哀鸿遍野寒鸦噪，
凄凄好孤伶。

站的地是他乡地，
见的人是他乡人；
无人修造少活计，
愁煞手艺人。

一日遇着王都司，
三代为官有金银；
去年新盖四合院，
需装修隔整。

多多拜上观世音，
走投无路遇救星；
订下合同帮王家，
暂且放宽心。

起早睡晚忙活路，
苦干苦做苦自身；
为挣几文血汗钱，
两头见星星。

刨花飞卷圈连圈，
锯末飞扬落纷纷；
忙得胡子理不赢，
张飞做老庚。

Sorrowful cries dominate the wild,
While ravens croak to sad souls.

Standing on unfamiliar soil,
Seeing no acquaintances,
No construction leads to no work,
Which worries the craftman.

Came across General Wang one day.
His family is rich for three generations in politics.
He built a new house last year,
And is now intending to decorate.

Worshipping Guanyin has worked,
And the star comes to my rescue.
I sign the contract,
And rest assured to help the Wang family.

I work day and night,
Day in and day out,
To earn a few coppers wrung from my blood,
I meet the star coming and going.

Wooden flakes fly about,
And powder hovers around.
I have no time to cut my beard,
Making myself a peer of Zhang Fei.

流云催着日月走，
惊蛰过了刮春风；
布谷声声报清明，
催人闹春耕。

手扳指头算一算，
一日离家一日深；
想必家乡望夫柳，
此时已发青。

我妻在家多困苦，
赡老养小度光阴；
盼我挣钱回家乡，
把重担减轻。

我也常把家小挂，
结算工钱想起身；
墨斗弹线直打直，
心往家乡奔。

都司是个笑面虎，
错把鹞子当鹦鹉；
错把老虎当观音，
害得我好苦。

一听我把工钱算，
设下陷阱埋下弩；
开出烂条把我害，
抽出杀人斧。

Drifting clouds steal the time.
After the Waking of Insects, the spring breeze comes.
Cuckoo calls announce Pure Brightness,
Urging people for spring sowing.

Counting the days with fingers,
I've been away from home for long.
Willows back home shall bud
At this time of year.

My wife at home bears bitter want—
Tending the elders, raising our brood.
And longing for my return
To share the burden.

I miss my family all the time,
And I'd finish up and return.
I'd use the marker for a straight line,
And head for home right away.

The Commander, a smiling tiger,
Takes the hawk for parrot,
The tiger for Guanyin.
And I'm the one who pays the price.

The moment I speak of wages,
He lays snares and buries crossbows;
He forges a rotten clause to ruin me,
Then whips out an axe for killing.

都司暴跳三丈高，
吹胡瞪眼手叉腰，
说是昨晚公子病，
一夜发高烧。

为退高烧泡金汁，
手箍煮在茶罐中；
今天早晨不见了，
一口赖我偷。

都司吼了太太叫，
说是手箍这一道，
上面镶着颗宝石，
价值几百吊。

若是我不交出来，
就把衙役皂吏叫；
她的男人王都司，
管五营四哨。

师爷开口细嗓门：
“都司府中无外人，
烧茶吃水只有你，
就你一个人。”

一口咬定是我偷，
要想分辩万不能；
不容我说一句话，
怎说也不行。

The Commander is angry,
Beard stiffened and hand around waist,
Saying that his son got ill last night,
And caught fever overnight.

To break the fever,
They boil soup with a golden bracelet
Which is gone the next morning.
And they claim that I stole it.

The General and his wife yell hard,
Saying that the bracelet
Is inlaid with diamond,
And worth a fortune.

If I don't hand over,
They'd send officials here.
Her husband, the Commander, is
In charge of five battalions.

The advisor says in low voice,
"There are no others inside,
Only you when boiling the soup.
And it'd be you, no doubt."

They insist that I stole,
And leave me no room for argument.
They won't let me talk,
Not even a word.

阳春三月刮黑风，
王家太爷怒气冲，
跺跺手杖来打我，
家丁来帮凶。

捆绑吊打不留情，
腰杆打得像张弓；
晴天霹雳遭冤屈，
有理说不通。

日出三丈昏沉沉，
王家老奶念经文，
敲罢木鱼走下楼，
姗姗下佛庭。

双眉一皱南无佛，
小嘴一弯就骂人；
骂我人穷骨头贱，
把我赶出门。

王家实在太凶残，
拉着黄牛便是马；
红嘴白牙诬害我，
昧心害忠良。

谁见你家金手箍，
分明是把工钱诳；
我人虽穷志不短，
不见也没拿。

Like black wind in March,
The elder Wang gets furious,
Trying to beat me with his stick,
Servants being his accomplices.

They tie me up
And beat me hard.
My body is tormented,
No hope for justice.

It is about noon.
The Commander's mother finishes her prayers
And walks downstairs
To the garden slowly.

With frown eyebrows,
She curses without mercy
That I am a poor of no spine.
She drives me out of the house.

The Wangs are indeed cruel,
Calling white black.
They frame me up
Without any mercy.

Who would have stolen your bracelet?
You are just too mean to extort payment.
Poor as I am,
I'd never steal.

白玉打烂还是玉，
瓦瓮虽全还是瓦；
男子无性铁无钢，
告他到大堂。

真火恼，
救命去把老虎找；
轻信官府如明镜，
自把苦来讨。

州官都司是亲家，
府官都司两相好；
自古官官两相护，
是非全颠倒。

原告反成了被告，
判我王家做家奴；
满腹冤情无处诉，
何日才出头。

星星赶月月赶星，
一日离家一日深；
硬赔手箍当娃子，
苦熬度光阴。

今年苦苦赔不够，
明年苦苦赔不清；
日望归雁常叹息，
夜里泪湿枕。

Broken jade is jade still,
And a tile remains a tile.
Man without character is iron without strength,
And I'd sue them in court.

What a joke!
I ask a tiger for help,
Believing that justice do exist.
I am just asking for trouble myself.

The magistrate and the Commander are relatives,
And the governor and the Commander are in good relation.
Officials protect officials,
Turning things upside down.

The plaintiff has become the defendant.
Sentencing me to serve as a household slave for the wang family;
Grievances nowhere to be heard,
When will this endless night end?

Stars chase after the moon,
Sorrow deepens every day away from home;
Forced to pay for the bracelet,
I endure bitterness and hardship.

One year's hard work isn't enough for the bracelet,
And I worry one more year won't be enough either.
Observing the returning wild geese,
I'd sigh and tears wet my pillow.

清明谷雨柳丝绿，
立夏小满雨纷纷；
柳青柳绿年复年，
凄凄布谷声。

七年八年困此地，
家小如何度光阴；
哪日不把家小挂，
夜夜到五更。

五更天做回乡梦，
未到乡境天已明；
失群孤雁天边叫，
声声箭穿心。

五、逃出虎口

翠莹莹，
太阳落了月亮升；
为出虎口拼命逃，
奔逃到三更。

大路宽宽不敢走，
小路弯弯刺蓬生；
闯过刺棵进老林，
山上阴森森。

忽闻耳边叮叮响，
好似白族三弦声；

Willows bud during Pure Brightness and Grain Rain.
It rains often during the Beginning of Summer and Grain Buds.
Willows turn green year by year.
The cuckoo cries sadly.

Trapped here for seven or eight years,
I wonder how my family would survive.
Not a single day do I stop thinking of them—
Each night I lie awake till the fifth watch.

I dream of returning home,
Yet the sun rises before my arrival.
The lonely wild goose cries in the distance—
Each cry like an arrow through the heart.

V. Escape

Bright and shining,
The sun sets, the moon rises;
To escape from the tiger's mouth,
I keep running till midnight.

Too risky to take the wide road,
I choose the tangled, thorn-wound track;
Breaking through the thorns,
I enter the desolate forest.

A tinkling sound enters my ears,
Like the sound of a three-stringed instrument;

平心静气抬头望，
看见一盏灯。

摸摸下巴打主意，
侧着耳朵细细听；
清风传来民家调，
传来白曲声。

一位老伯灯下坐，
怀中三弦响叮叮；
望月长歌思乡曲，
句句动我心。

多年不闻家乡曲，
如今听着倍觉亲；
原来也是出门人，
打野在山阴。

饱含热泪奔上前，
苦情诉给乡亲听；
同是天涯沦落人，
他乡遇知音。

乡亲听我沦落情，
个个双目泪淋淋；
牙根咬得咯咯响，
人人鸣不平。

Calmly and quietly, I raise my head,
And see a flickering light.

Rubbing my chin,
I listen carefully;
The gentle breeze brings over
The wonderful tune of a Bai folk song.

An old man sits under the light,
Playing a three-stringed instrument,
Singing a song of homesickness,
Each sentence of which moves my heart.

Having not heard hometown melodies for long,
I soon feel a profound bond;
It turns out we are both wanderers
Seeking a livelihood away from home.

Filled with tears, I rush over
To talk with my fellows;
We are all stranded souls on a foreign land,
Finding kindred spirits in a distant place.

After hearing my story,
They all burst into tears;
With extreme anger,
They express discontent.

忽然山下人马叫，
都司带兵来捉人；
火把点得通天亮，
山脚扎下营。

山神老伯定主意，
手捋胡须观山形；
吩咐大家心莫慌，
快快撒"米城"。

撒罢米城诵《木经》，
霎时山林雾腾腾；
烟雾茫茫不见月，
对面不见人。

砍来山楸雕龙头，
龙身龙爪紫金藤；
木刀木枪和木马，
几十木头人。

苍松下面设祭坛，
开光点主念咒文；
柏枝蘸水请鲁班，
即刻就显灵。

青龙翻滚下山去，
吼声隆隆如雷霆；
木人木马齐出阵，
进敌老营。

People soon gather below the mountain,
And the Commander is here to capture me;
Torches illuminate the night sky,
And they camp at the mountain foot.

The old mountain god soon has an idea,
Stroking his beard and observing the terrain;
He instructs everyone not to panic,
And make the "rice city" pattern quick.

He then recites the *Wood Sutra*,
And the forest is soon filled with dense fog;
The fog covers up the moon,
And people are unable to see others.

Cut mountain ash for dragon heads,
Coil purple-gold vines for bodies and claws.
Carve wooden blades, wooden lances, wooden steeds,
And a whole troop of timber warriors.

The altar stands under the pine trees,
Where ritual is performed and mantras are chanted;
Cypress branches are dipped in water to invite Lu Ban—
And before the words are done, his spirit is here.

The green dragon rolls down the mountain,
Its roar resounding like thunder;
The wooden soldiers and horses march in formation,
Advancing towards the enemy's camp.

黑烟腾腾山岳动，
杀声阵阵如雷霆；
三更杀到五更过，
一夜到天明。

都司兵马被打败，
乡亲救我出火坑；
举手频频长相揖，
谢谢老山神。

辞别众位想回去，
身上银钱无半文；
只因手长衣袖短，
实在好伤情。

请求山神收容我，
跟着众位下龙陵；
等我挣了几文钱，
慢慢再回程。

六、傣家留客

龙陵、镇康下盈江，
傣家地方好风光；
青山绿水绕村寨，
云深树苍苍。

Black smoke billows, shaking the hills;
War-cries crash like rolling thunder.
From the third watch on they slash past the fifth,
And the battle keeps raging till dawn.

The Commander is defeated,
And I am saved;
I raise my hands and bow,
To thank the old mountain god.

After farewell, I'd head home,
Yet without money in my pockets;
Without a proper dress,
It is indeed a heartbreaking situation.

Mountain god, take me in—
Let me march down to Longling with the rest.
Once I've earned a few coppers,
I'll find my slow way home.

VI. Hospitality of the Dai Family

From Longling and Zhenkang down to Yingjiang:
Dai land, a realm of beauty.
Green hills ring the villages, clear waters flow,
Clouds hang thick, and dense dark trees rise.

竹楼间间依山盖，
龙竹蓬蓬映水乡；
一年四季花不败，
冬天也无霜。

世间此地时令好，
边收稻谷边栽秧；
一年两熟丰足地，
算得鱼米乡。

土司住的青瓦房，
富丽堂皇美女窗；
柱脚楼台雕龙凤，
无板不雕花。

一脚踏进盈江坝，
山神誉满傣人家；
人人口称大山神，
家家请相帮。

这家要做小方桌，
那家要雕格子窗；
有的请漆雕花床，
有的做衣箱。

布谷声声叫清明，
正想收拾登归程；
来了一位大佛爷，
留住不放行：

Bamboo houses nestle in the mountains,
And dragon bamboo reflects in the water;
Flowers bloom all year round,
And there is no frost even in winter.

Here the seasons are good:
Rice is cut while the next shoot is set;
Two harvests a year load every barn—
A land where fish swim and rice grows.

The chieftain resides in a tiled house,
With magnificent hails and beautiful windows;
Dragon and phoenix carvings adorn the pillars,
No planks are left without intricate designs.

Stepping into Yingjiang Dam,
The mountain god is popular;
They praise him,
Seeking his assistance.

Some wants him to make a small table,
Some requests a carved window;
Some asks for lacquered beds,
While some longs for a wardrobe for clothes.

The cuckoo cry indicates Pure Brightness,
When I am about to pack up and return home,
An old man comes over
To stop me from leaving.

"本地要盖新缅寺，
长老景慕山神名；
恭请山神去画墨，
请立马登程。

"久闻山神手艺巧，
土木之工动鬼神；
十八文钱摆两路，
九文又九文。"

说完打开黄筒帕，
拿出杏黄纸公文；
指名要叫山神去，
不去也不成。

知恩不报非君子，
终生难忘山神情；
忍心打消回乡意，
伴山神同行。

傣家长老不放行，
大伙只得去应承；
架马出料摆场子，
马上动工程。

人说木匠状元才，
山神掌墨如有神；
大墨小墨顶纯熟，
最有条有井。

"We are building a new temple.
The master admires the mountain god
And insists to ask him for help.
Please hit the road right away.

"I have long heard
The name of the mountain god,
And I'd invite him over
Whatever it takes."

He then opens a yellow cloth,
And takes out an official document,
Requesting help from the mountain god.
It's not an option to negotiate.

A gentleman repays every kindness—
The mountain god's grace I swear to keep
I crush my longing for homecoming,
And walk beside him through the peaks.

The Dai master won't let go,
And we have to agree.
We take out the tools,
And start the project immediately.

People say carpenters are talents
And the mountain god's expertise is excellent;
Skillful in ink markers,
He works meticulously.

大料小料三千件，
肥梁瘦柱好分明；
四面出水转景楼，
大殿分二层。

七梁八角十六柱，
凤角飞檐吊金铃；
鳌鱼含脊两山扬，
莲花托宝顶。

腾龙抱柱现三节，
流云捧月有分明；
檐下层层架斗拱，
斗斗有花纹。

挂方照面雕如意，
前后透漏“卍”字形；
大插京枋龙抬头，
昂首有精神。

厅堂格子三层花，
雕的西天极乐境；
比丘、罗汉盘腿坐，
佛祖讲经文。

祥云朵朵佛光照，
古树枯藤挂峻岭；
唐僧师徒山间走，
西天取经文。

Numerous pieces of materials are
Used for thick beams and slender pillars;
A building soon appears,
With a grand hall and two stories.

Beams and columns,
Are intricately decorated;
Turtle-shaped ridges with raised spines,
And lotus flower supports the top.

Flying dragons embrace the pillars,
And flowing clouds dwell around the moon;
Brackets stack beneath the eaves,
Every joint adorned with figures.

"Ruyi" symbols carved,
"Swastika" pattern hollowed,
The large dragon head is designed
With a spirited presence.

Three layers of lattice patterns in the hall are
Carved to depict the blissful realm of the Western Paradise;
Monks and Arhats sit cross-legged,
While Buddha preaches scriptures.

Buddha's light shines through auspicious clouds.
Ancient trees and withered vines hang from steep mountains.
Master Tang and his disciples walk in the mountains,
Embarking on the journey to the Western Paradise.

唐僧厚重如佛像，
悟空狡狡真机灵；
似痴非痴猪八戒，
沙僧心最诚。

走廊转廊通曲径，
清泉潺潺绕凉亭；
翠竹蓬蓬摇绿影，
好似绿风屏。

门前一对石狮子，
一蹲一卧真传神；
红漆柱子红如朱，
油亮黑漆门。

缅塔宝顶闪金辉，
幢幢矗立高入云；
金钟声声山谷应，
赛蓬莱仙境。

长老见了点头笑，
佛爷个个喜盈盈；
埋头做活忘年月，
转眼一年整。

此地不是终老处，
日暮黄昏动乡情；
去辞山神老伯伯，
我欲登归程。

Master Tang is as solemn as a Buddha statue.
Wukong the monkey is clever and cunning.
Pigsy is pretending to be foolish.
Sha Wujing is most sincere.

Corridors and walkways wind about.
Clear stream runs around pavilions.
Bamboo shadow sways,
Like a green windscreen.

There is a pair of stone lions in front of the gate,
One squatting and the other lying;
Lacquered pillars are as red as cinnabar,
And black lacquered doors shine.

Golden spires of the pagodas flash with light,
Tower after tower soaring into the clouds;
Every bronze bell carries its note through the valleys—
A realm that outshines the Isles of the Blest.

The old master nods and smiles.
Joy blooms on every one's face.
Working here day in and day out,
And it's already one year.

I shall not grow old here.
At dusk, nostalgia strikes me.
I bid farewell to the mountain god,
Intending to embark on my journey home.

山神劝我莫匆匆，
稍等缅寺盖成功；
长老也来挽留我，
留我过残冬。

正月十五采花会，
恰逢缅寺正竣工；
傣人家家来赕佛，
来去闹哄哄。

佛爷奏起开堂乐，
笙箫琴笛伴磬钟；
香火缭绕绿荫里，
袅袅飘半空。

青年男女相邀约，
采花献佛又打歌；
铓锣声声孔雀舞，
象脚鼓咚咚。

堆沙听经青草坪，
泼水相戏花房中；
秋千飞荡绿荫里，
赛船与丢包。

香蕉、粽子相馈赠，
槟榔、罗子一封封；
芭蕉叶包糯米饭，
相敬如弟兄。

The mountain god advises me not to rush,
And wait till the completion of the temple;
Even the master tries to persuade me,
To stay till the coming spring.

On the Lantern Festival,
The temple is completed;
Folks come here to pay tribute,
And it is quite a busy scene.

Music starts in the hall,
Accompanied by flutes, pipes, lutes, and bells;
Incense smoke lingers,
Gently drifting in the air.

Young men and maidens pair by pair,
Pluck blossoms for the Buddha, then burst into songs;
Nuo-gongs shimmer, peacocks wheel,
and elephant-foot drums roll like thunder.

On green lawns they heap bright sand and listen to the sutras,
In petal-decked pavilions they splash each other with water;
Swings fly through the shade,
While boats race and embroidered love-bags sail through the air.

Bananas and zongzi are exchanged as gifts.
Areca nuts and betel leaves are wrapped.
With sticky rice wrapped in banana leaves,
We respect each other like brothers.

高升飞入半天云，
响如霹雳震苍穹；
人夜还放孔明灯，
腾腾入太空。

大青树下竹笛响，
男女双双入林中；
轻歌如丝悠悠来，
明月照苍松。

此时明月家乡同，
挂老挂小挂家中；
离别家乡十多年，
音信久不通。

辞别山神和众位，
归心似箭扎痛胸；
结算工钱登归程，
一路乘长风。

There are performers high up in the sky.
Thunder cracks across the trembling sky.
Some people fly the Kongming lanterns,
Which rise up into the vast space.

Bamboo flutes are played under the green tree,
While valentines date in the forest;
Their voices rise, soft as silk on midnight air—
While the bright moon shines on green pines.

The moon back home shall be the same.
I miss my family members so much.
It's been more than ten years;
No word has crossed the mountain since.

Bidding farewell to all,
I can't wait to go home.
After settlling the wages,
I rush way home.

出门恋歌

一、初见

男：见到阿妹我心慌，
新衣新帕巧梳妆，
转过头来偷看我，
笑笑情意长。
千人指戳我不怕，
惹出是非我承担，
世上哪个不谈情，
问她去何方。

女：阿哥上山我下山，
哥妹相遇路中间，
哥妹相遇路当头，
相望情绵绵。
阿哥望我眼圈红，
我望阿哥红了脸，
燕子也要做夫妻，
想和哥攀连。

Love Song of Going Outside

I. First Sight

M: I fluster first time seeing you
Dressed in new clothes, breathtaking.
You turn around and peep at me,
Smiling like a flower.
I fear no more,
Being ready to take on the world.
Man is to love.
I asked where is she heading.

F: You climb the mountain while I descend,
Midway we meet on the winding road.
Face to face where the path turns steep.
Looking at each other,
Your eyes turn red,
While I blush.
Swallows live in pairs,
And I'd like to be the one for you.

男：领褂你穿灯草绒，
漂白衣裳玉镯头，
阿妹好比耀眼花，
说话带笑容。
阿哥爱你好身材，
阿哥爱你情意浓，
有缘千里来相会，
蜜蜂遇花丛。

女：阿哥属羊好身手，
漂白衣裳白包头，
说两句话笑三笑，
生来多温柔。
阿妹爱你身材好，
阿妹想你日子久，
看你为人多勤劳，
爱得难开口。

男：梅子花开东江头，
阿哥有意把你求，
喝你花上甜露水，
在你花边守。
太阳出来常相会，
月亮东升又发愁，
白天相见晚相别，
夜夜梦中游。

M: Dressed in spotless velvet coat,
And wearing jade ornaments,
Little sister, you dazzle like brilliant flowers.
Every word you speak comes with a smile.
I love your graceful figure,
And your deep affection.
Fate brings us together across a thousand miles—
Like bees meeting a whole bank of blossoms.

F: My lad, born in the Year of the Ram, swift and strong,
your spotless turban and jacket gleam white;
You talk with soft laughters—
Such gentle ways you're born with.
I love your fine frame.
I have longed for you day after day;
Seeing how hard you work, how kind you are,
Love fills my throat—too full for words.

M: Plum blossoms open along the eastern river—
I come with longing to claim your heart.
Let me sip the sweet dew from your petals
And keep watch at the edge of your bloom.
When the sun climbs we meet without end;
When the moon climbs I'm left with longing.
Daylight brings us together, night drives us apart—
Yet every dark hour we wander together in dreams.

女：新织衣，
春来柳丝长绿须，
哥妹扯动牵心绳，
全身冒热气。
大风吹散乌云层，
太阳照热深水区，
哥妹扯动牵心绳，
扯得心欢喜。

二、定情

男：一更月亮含山嘴，
阿妹有情心灵美，
阿哥空背你花名，
你心给了谁？
天上三星跟北斗，
河里鱼儿不离水，
哥是春牛没有伴，
伤心无人陪。

女：二更月亮已照高，
阿哥何必把心焦，
好花迟早给你摘，
阿哥莫心焦。
手上金镯留给你，
情意两头一肩挑，
年纪长到二十四，
也该绽花苞。

F: New clothes woven,
Spring's willow threads dance in the breeze.
Brother and sister pull the heartstrings tight.
Our bodies flush with a fever of love.
The gale scatters the dark clouds;
The sun warms the deep waters—
Brother and sister pull the heartstrings tight,
Our hearts swell with unspoken joy.

II. Promise

M: The moon rises from the mountain at the first watch.
You have a beautiful soul,
And I call your name in vain.
Who's won your heart?
Three stars follow the Big Dipper in the sky.
Fish in the river never leave the water.
I am a spring ox without a mate,
So sad, with no one to keep me company.

F: The moon climbs high at the second watch,
No need to fret, my dear,
The finest blooms are yet to be picked—
So calm your anxious heart.
These golden bracelets, I leave for you,
Our bond, we'll shoulder together.
Now twenty-four, I've come of age—
It's time to blossom.

男：三更月亮已当顶，
独自伤悲孤零零，
流不完的相思泪，
哪个来同情？
阿妹虽然常相见，
是否爱我不应承？
太阳出来霜雪化，
怕妹去无影。

女：四更月亮已偏西，
我不答应哥不依，
这样许愿嫌不够，
盟誓跪在地。
当天对地给你说，
相爱百年不分离，
哥妹相好到百岁，
把心掏给你。

男：五更月亮落西山，
阿妹答应哥喜欢，
阿妹把心掏给哥，
信物把心拴。
抑或剪给头发辫，
抑或玉镯和手绢，
相爱就要有诚意，
爱情意志坚。

M: The moon hangs right up in the sky at the third watch,
While I sit sad and alone,
Tears filling my eyes.
Who would sympathize with me?
Although we meet often,
Do you love me?
I am afraid when the sun comes out,
You'd be gone.

F: The moon falls a bit to the west at the fourth watch,
And you won't give up till I say yes.
If a promise isn't good enough,
I'll kneel and take an oath.
I'll say to you, right here, right now,
I'll love you for a hundred years,
I'll be with you till the end,
I'll give you my heart.

M: The moon falls down the mountain at the fifth watch.
I am glad that you've agreed and
Give your heart to me.
I ask a love token from you,
Be it a bunch of hair,
A bracelet or a handkerchief.
Love must be sincere,
With a strong will.

女：悠悠忆，
你要信物也容易，
哥要什么妹给你，
阿妹随哥意。
把头靠在哥怀里，
随哥剪我头发辫，
用它做你随身伴，
陪着阿哥去。

男：花朵新，
人才也美情也深，
品德纯真白如雪，
两眼亮晶晶。
世间遇过多少人，
阿妹算得女能人，
阿哥采着金桂花，
死了也甘心。

女：金雀鸟，
阿哥为人谁不晓？
能写会算讲道理，
乡里名声好。
能文能武有才气，
打着火把也难找，
阿妹有眼识泰山，
才愿跟哥好。

F: Sweet memories!
That's so easy.
I'll give you whatever you ask.
I'll follow your heart's desire.
I'll rest my head on your chest.
Let you cut my hair,
So you can keep it
by your side.

M: Fresh Flowers!
You have talent and beauty, as well as deep affection.
Pure as snow, your character has shown.
Eyes that sparkle, bright as dawn,
Met many people in this life,
No one compares to you, my love.
If I could have you by my side,
I'd die a happy man.

F: Golden oriole!
Who doesn't know you?
You are wise and reasonable,
And well-known in the village.
Talented in both literature and martial arts,
You are one of those hard-to-find.
I have eyes to see your worth.
That's why I am willing to follow you.

三、起誓

男：石宝飞泉崖下流，
哥妹相爱才开头，
哥妹相好人嫉妒，
难封众人口。
我们分手他高兴，
我们相爱他记仇，
就像钉子扎他眼，
灌他喝苦酒。

女：哥妹采花相碰头，
金剪刀剪绿花绸，
就算有人说闲话，
没装心里头。
人多地方偏要去，
没有人时手牵手，
村头巷尾常相见，
笑笑也解愁。

男：小妹娣，
火候到时松油滴，
我俩花柳成夫妻，
石头现水底。
夜长梦多要注意，
嫉妒那人中伤你，
抑或爹妈不同意，
绝对不分离。

III. Taking the Oath

M: The waterfall flows over the cliffs.
Our love has just begun.
Jealousy fills the air.
Gossip can't be held back.
They'd be glad if we part,
They'd be bitter if we stay.
It's like a nail in their eyes.
They drink the bitter wine.

F: We go together to pick flowers,
Snip green silk with golden shears.
Even if people gossip,
We don't let it weigh on our hearts.
We'll go where the crowds are,
And hold hands when no one's around.
We meet often in the village lanes,
A smile can chase away all our cares.

M: My pretty girl,
When the time is ripe,
We'll marry and be a couple,
And let things settle.
You shall be careful at nights,
Because those who are jealous may hurt you.
Even if our parents disagree,
We will not split up.

女：有情哥，
两个脑袋心一颗，
两个身子一条命，
不怕路坎坷。
爹妈反对要说服，
相交不怕是非多，
故意做给他们瞧，
不怕起风波。

男：阿妹有情我有意，
有情有意同路行，
有情有意才相遇，
相好一路行。
你说相爱到牙缺，
我说爱到白发人，
和你相爱到百岁，
相依共温存。

女：有情哥呀，
爱情千万莫做假，
要是阿哥怀假意，
你怕雷打？
妹子只是弱女子，
真心实意谁不亏，
假情假意无廉耻，
真情莫做假。

F: My dear brother,
Two heads, one heart,
Two bodies, one shared fate.
We shall not fear the rugged path.
We will persuade our parents,
No matter how much they oppose.
We'll show them what we're made of,
And let no stormy waves deter us.

M: Oh, my girl!
We are destined to meet,
To love and
To be together forever.
You said let us love till we lose our teeth,
And I'd say till our hairs turn gray.
My love for you shall last a century
And never fade away.

F: Oh, my dear brother!
Love should never be feigned.
If you hold false intentions,
Aren't you afraid of thunder strikes?
I am but a tragile girl,
Please treat me with honesty.
False love is shameful.
True love should never be a trick.

男：对天对地把头磕，
当对日月盟誓约，
如果我要有假心，
短命不得活。
子弹从我脑里过，
刀子在我心上落，
如果我要有假心，
短命不得活。

女：长流水，
真心相爱头莫回，
海水干了情不断，
山崩心不悔。
人说人生路难走，
千山万水有高低，
人生难走坎坷路，
手牵手相随。

四、别离

男：我给阿妹吐真情，
伙伴约我去出门，
伙伴约我出门去，
去几天才行。
平时家里开销多，
手里无钱事难成，
将来和你结成亲，
才有好光景。

M: I'll kneel and knock my head on the ground,
And swear to the sun and the moon.
If I have a false heart,
I shall die young,
A bullet through my brain,
A knife in my heart.
If I have a false heart,
I shall die young.

F: The river keeps flowing.
True love never looks back.
Love till the ocean dries,
Even if mountains collapse.
People say life is hard,
Mountains high, rivers wide,
Life is full of bumps and hurdles,.
Hand in hand, we'll stride.

IV. Separation

M: I must be honest with you, my girl.
A friend of mine
Invites me to go out,
For just a couple of days.
Family expenses are high.
I need to make more money
To marry you in the future
And live a better life.

女：听说阿哥要出门，
阿妹给哥说分明，
伙伴约你出门去，
明年再出行。
不找钱财只一次，
只要日子过安宁，
哥妹才是新相好，
难割相思情。

男：要去出门难动身，
离别情妹丢知音，
路上高山难爬过，
阿妹又牵心。
要爬高山大又险，
要过坝子远又深，
山高路远又想你，
出门多艰辛。

女：阿哥出门把衣洗，
阿妹收拾来送你，
怎么说也送你去，
送你到大理。
拉你左手来祝愿，
拉你右手话别离，
阿哥出门顶南风，
月圆心里虚。

F: I hear you are going out.
I need to make things clear.
Your friend asks you to go out,
But can't it wait till next year?
Skip making money this time,
As long as we live in peace.
We've just been together,
I can't bear this lovesickness.

M: It's hard for me to go,
To leave my love behind.
The mountains are hard to climb,
And you'll be worried for me.
The mountains are high and steep,
The valleys are far and deep,
With every step, I'll think of you,
Though the journey is tough.

F: I'll wash your clothes clean,
And pack up for you.
I'll see you off, no matter what,
To Dali, if you dare.
I'll hold your left hand to wish you well,
Your right hand to say farewell.
You'll travel against the southern wind,
I'll feel empty when the moon is round.

男：阿妹情意似海深，
送你银锁带在身，
金钥匙能开银锁，
锁住你花心。
有人买花你莫卖，
莫让钱财迷眼睛，
世上钱财是粪土，
情意值千金。

女：阿哥出门准备走，
送你送到南门口，
送你送到南门外，
眼泪四股流。
阿哥难把双脚迈，
阿妹等哥到多久，
心想再叫哥一声，
怕哥又回头。

男：心忧忧，
为了出门把妹丢，
刚刚走到半路上，
哭声把心揪。
阿妹哭来哥心疼，
麻绳绊脚心难收，
哥心难随身子去，
心被妹子勾。

M: My love for you is as deep as the sea.
I'll give you a silver lock to wear.
A golden key will unlock it,
To keep your heart from straying.
If someone tries to buy your love, don't sell,
Don't let money blind your eyes.
See money as dirt,
True love is worth more than gold.

F: You're ready to go,
I'll see you off
At the southern gate.
With tears streaming down my face,
You take your steps,
And I start my endless wait.
I want to call your name once more,
But fear you'll turn back, and I can't bear.

M: I feel so worried
To leave you behind.
Halfway down the road,
Your crying breaks my heart.
I ache, hearing you cry.
My feet feel tied, can't go on.
My heart can't go with my body,
It stays with you, forever bound.

女：有情哥，
清清池水起风波，
女子生来心肠软，
情思搅心窝。
妹我仔细来思量，
抓夫派役捐税多，
穿衣吃饭都要钱，
哥腿不能拖。

男：说你听，
钱财虽薄情意深，
为了要过好日子，
出门把钱挣。
阿妹心中莫难过，
树叶般日子数不清，
大雁南飞我也回，
阿妹莫伤心。

女：哥有情，
送哥送到大理城，
走到大理街子上，
与哥吃点心。
阿哥下酒吃肉片，
妹撒草果五香粉，
人看我俩双飞雁，
谁知各飞腾。

F: My dear brother,
The clear pond's surface ripples with the wind.
Girls are soft-hearted by nature.
My heart is disturbed.
I've thought it over carefully:
Many are conscripted, and taxes still weigh,
Clothing and meals all cost money,
You really can't afford to delay.

M: Listen to me.
Though money's thin, my love runs deep.
To live a better life,
I'll go out and earn what we need.
Don't let sorrow fill your heart.
The days ahead are countless, like leaves.
When geese fly south, I'll come back,
So don't be sad.

F: My dear brother,
I'll see you off to Dali.
Stroll the streets with you,
Share a meal, enjoy the view.
You'll sip wine, savor meat.
I'll sprinkle cardamom and five-spice powder.
Onlookers see us as a pair of geese,
Who'd guess we'll part, no care.

男：身背三弦要起身，
妹和女伴快回村，
梁祝十八里相送，
终究要离分。
阿妹你要买什么，
仔细说给阿哥听，
收拾东西哥去了，
伙伴把我等。

女：有情哥，
妹要阿哥心一颗，
荣华富贵不羡慕，
只要贴心窝。
哥走无人贴心暖，
知心话儿对谁说，
阿哥快去快些回，
莫让花凋落。

五、相思

男：花上花，
出门好久不回家，
有情小妹丢后头，
心里乱如麻。
我像孤雁飞朝南，
哪天与妹合成双？
天上月牙何时圆？
回家闻花香。

M: With my lute on my back, I'm ready to leave.
My love and her friend quickly return to the village.
Though you see me off for miles, like Liang and Zhu,
In the end, we must part.
My dear, what do you wish to buy?
Let me know in detail.
I'll pack my things and be on my way.
My friend is waiting for me.

F: My dear brother
I want your whole heart,
Not wealth or fame,
Just to be in your mind.
When you're alone, with no one to confide,
Who will you talk to, who will be your guide?
Come back soon, don't delay,
Don't let love fade away.

V. Lovesickness

Flowers bloom on flowers.
I've been away for so long,
Left my beloved behind,
My heart's in turmoil.
I'm like a lonely wild goose flying south.
When will I be reunited with my love?
When will the crescent moon be full?
I long to return, to breathe the scent of home.

女：柳下花，
自从阿哥离了家，
衣裳脏了懒得洗，
吃饭胃口差。
铺垫再多难睡好，
翻来覆去睡不下，
想起蜜蜂离花丛，
两眼含泪花。

男：思念情，
不好开口让人听，
不好开口对人讲，
说给月和星。
我请三星说给你，
我求北斗传音信，
多谢三星和北斗，
发点慈善心。

女：小金蜂，
替我给哥诉苦心，
阿哥他虽想念我，
为何不回村？
园里红花把蜂等，
蜜蜂不来采花心，
叫我阿哥快回来，
花开等蜜蜂。

F: Flowers beneath the willow.
Ever since you left home,
I'm too lazy to wash my clothes,
And my appetite's gone.
I can't sleep sound,
Tossing and turning all night long.
Like a bee away from the flowers,
My eyes are filled with tears.

M: My longing,
Hard to speak,
Hard to share,
So I whisper to the moon and stars.
I ask the stars to tell you.
I beg the Dipper to send my words.
I am extremely grateful
For the kindness of the Dipper and stars.

F: Little golden bee,
Carry my sorrows, please.
Though he misses me,
Why won't he come home?
The red flowers in the garden wait for the bees,
But the bees don't come to sip their nectar.
Tell him to come back home soon.
The flowers are waiting for the bees.

男：听见蜜蜂叫嗡嗡，
它说阿妹把我等，
它说阿妹思念我，
梦里也相亲。
梦见七仙遇董永，
梦见许仙配蛇精，
梦见牛郎和织女，
七夕会知音。

女：阿哥出门在南方，
头上乌云遮阳光，
风吹乌云散去后，
何时做一双？
心想身子寄哥旁，
一时飞来到你方，
可惜阿妹年纪轻，
难到哥身旁。

男：往北瞧，
瞧见阿妹朝南跑，
瞧见阿妹来找我，
把我肩膀摇。
本来不应离开你，
本来不该把你抛，
河里鱼儿跟水游，
顺水把哥找。

M: I hear the bees buzz.
They say my love waits for me,
Missing me so much,
Seeing me in her dreams.
I dream of Dong Yong with the fairy,
Xu Xian with the white snake,
Niu Lang with Zhinv,
All meeting on the Chinese Valentine's Day.

F: My dear, you're in the south.
Beneath dark clouds, you strive.
Once the winds clear those clouds away,
When will you return to me?
I wish I could fly to your side,
In a moment, just like that.
But I'm too young
To reach you.

M: Looking to the north,
And there you are, running towards me,
Seeking me out,
Shaking my shoulders with glee.
I never should have gone,
Left you all alone.
Like a fish follows the stream,
You come to me, a dream.

女：往南瞧，
阿哥身影真难找，
阿哥身影难找到，
一直往南瞧。
兰花开在南山顶，
兰花躲进野山坳，
纵虽阿哥找不到，
我也向南找。

六、疑云

男：月亮出来含山嘴，
饭后散心到村尾，
一时之间想起妹，
心头浇凉水。
桥下河水清如油，
山间明月比雪美，
我对山水问一句：
阿妹可后悔？

女：乌云朵朵遮月光，
想来想去好心伤，
有情阿哥出门去，
还不回家乡。
怕是乌云遮他眼，
采着牡丹在他乡，
山盟海誓风吹散，
安家在远方。

F: Looking to the south,
You are so hard to find,
So hard to find,
Yet I keep looking.
The orchids bloom on the mountaintops.
The orchids hide in the wild valleys.
Even though you are hard to find,
I still look to the south.

VI. Doubts

M: The moon comes out.
I take a walk to the end of the village after dinner.
For a moment, I think of you.
And My heart feels so cold.
Water under the bridge is so clear.
The bright moon in the mountains is more bealltiful than snow.
I ask the mountains and the water,
"My dear, do you ever regret?"

F: Dark clouds hide the moonlight,
And I feel so sad.
My beloved has left home,
And he hasn't come back yet.
I'm afraid dark clouds have blinded his eyes.
He might have found another love in a faraway place.
The vows we made have been blown away by the wind,
And he has settled down far away.

男：昨夜梦境伤我心，
梦见阿妹去会亲，
阿妹接着厚彩礼，
要准备成婚。
早知姑娘怀假意，
何必当初表坚贞，
花柳好似玉冰块，
饿了吃不成。

女：好伤心，
阿哥喝了疯药汤，
阿哥陷进泥塘里，
回不了家乡。
出门时节说好话，
大雁南飞回家乡，
出门三年不见回，
气坏我心肠。

男：做梦不知吉与凶，
常把阿妹挂心中，
和妹相处金镶玉，
豆腐拌青葱。
阿妹和我发过誓，
谁要反悔遭雷轰，
人眼不亮天眼亮，
善始要善终。

M: Last night's dream hurts my heart.
You were meeting someone else.
You were receiving expensive gifts,
And getting ready to get married.
If I had known you were insincere from the start,
Why did you pretend to be so loyal?
Flowers are like jade,
But you can't eat them when you're hungry.

F: Pretty sad.
Is my beloved man crazy,
Or stuck in the mud,
And unable to come home?
He said when we separated
That he would return when wild geese fly south.
It's been three years,
And I am heartbroken.

M: Good or bad the dream is,
I always have you in my heart.
I'd be with you like gold inlaid with jade,
Like tofu mixed with green onions.
We've taken an oath,
Whoever breaks it will be struck by thunder.
If people's eyes are blind, the heavens' eyes are not,
We must stay together till the end.

女：莫猜疑，
阿哥知书又识礼，
我和阿哥心换心，
他不会反悔。
阿哥出门顶风浪，
阿哥出门历艰险，
阿哥不回有原因，
他心清如水。

七、重逢

男：听见枝头喜鹊声，
怕是喜气降我身，
要是阿妹来接我，
手牵手回村。
燕子双双飞朝北，
衔泥衔草两相跟，
一双春牛同下田
一同闹春耕。

女：阿哥情意妹难忘，
盘缠寄到哥身旁，
寄给阿哥一封信，
把真心话讲。
栽秧季节快回来，
田里豆麦已发黄，
栽种节令只几天，
莫误好时光。

F: Don't doubt.
You are educated and know the customs.
We love each other.
He won't break his promise.
He's out there, facing storms.
He's out there, endaring hardships.
There must be a reason he hasn't come back.
But I know his heart is true.

VII. Reunion

M: I hear the magpies chattering,
And I wonder if good fortune is coming my way.
Could it be that my beloved is coming for me,
To take me home, hand in hand?
The swallows fly north in pairs,
Building nests together, side by side.
A pair of oxen in the spring, we'll go to the fields,
And farm in the spring together.

F: Your love is etched in my heart.
I'm sending you some money for the road.
I've also written you a letter,
To share my deepest thoughts with you.
Come back in time for the planting season.
The wheat in the fields is ripe and golden.
The planting season won't last long.
Don't let this precious time slip away.

男：三月清明赶回程，
枝头布谷叫得紧，
庄稼涌起黄金浪，
秧苗绿莹莹。
眼睛东望又西望，
眼睛南寻又北寻，
阿妹不来不怪她，
花间一回亲。

女：报春花，
阿哥出门转回家，
拿来明柴点把火，
照照他脸瓜。
去时脸似桃花色，
回来却像枯菜花，
阿哥得了什么病？
我放心不下。

男：不好意思说你听，
为你日夜牵我心，
白天做活把你想，
长夜梦五更。
梦见哥妹相依靠，
梦见两手握得紧，
醒过来时不见你，
伤心筋骨疼。

M：I'll return home in March.
Cuckoos cry hard on the branch.
The crops rise like waves of gold.
The seedlings are bright green.
I search from east and west,
North to south.
If she doesn't come, I won't complain,
For I'd see her among flowers.

F：Spring flower blooms.
My dear has returned home.
I'll take a burning stick,
To see his face clearly.
His face was like a peach blossom when he left,
But now it's as dark as withered cabbage.
What illness has my dear caught?
I can't stop worrying.

M：I feel shy to say it,
But I've been thinking of you day and night.
I think of you while working in the day,
And dream of you deep into night.
I dream that we are together,
Holding hands so tight.
But when I wake up, you are not there,
And my heart aches with sorrow.

女：当然想，
相思病人脸发黄，
蜜蜂飞回花丛里，
欢乐在花房。

男女：出门回来不再去，
一双蝴蝶采花忙，
时时刻刻不分离，
终老情更长。

F：Of course，
Lovesickness brings people illness.
Bees are flying around the flowers，
And dancing joyously in the cottage.

Chorus：Don't go out ever again.
Let us be a pair of butterflies，
Harvest around the flowers
And stay together forever.

巧 木 匠

一、漂泊异乡

漾江水畔四季青，
一片梨园绿莹莹。
有幢简陋的茅屋，
搭在梨树间。

屋里住着两代人，
一老一小爷孙俩。
爷爷人叫穷骨头，
孙孙名阿杏。

绳索偏从细处断，
恶狗偏咬穷苦人。
阿杏八岁爹娘死，
变成孤苦人。

近水的人知鱼性，
靠山的人识鸟音。
阿杏尝够人世苦，
从小心眼明。

The Skilled Carpenter

I. Away from Home

It is evergreen by the river of Yangjiang,
And the pear orchard is lush and green.
There's a simple thatched cottage
Built among the pear trees.

Inside the cottage
A grandfather and a grandson live.
The grandfather is called Poorbone,
And the grandson Axing.

A rope breaks at the weakest point,
And the vicious dog bites the poor.
Axing's parents died when he was eight,
Leaving him an orphan.

Those close to the water know the nature of fish.
Those living on the mountains recognize the sounds of birds.
Axing has tasted the bitterness of life,
And has been wise since childhood.

鸟飞千里靠翅膀，
人无手艺难做人。
阿杏决心学木匠，
造就好本领。

三三九十个夜晚，
三三九十个白天。
阿杏心灵手脚勤，
学得好手艺。

阿杏雕刻的木龙，
扬头甩尾戏明珠。
阿杏雕刻的凤凰，
飞翔在天空。

有志之人事竟成，
两支红烛放光彩。
师徒道别共晚宴，
互敬酒三杯。

师父斟的出师酒，
徒弟敬的报恩杯。
杯杯美酒分外甜，
师徒情不断。

辞别恩人要出门，
阿杏跪在师父前。
千言万语难出口，
泪水如流泉。

Birds fly thousands of miles relying on their wings.
Without skills, people are hard to survive.
Axing determines to learn carpentry,
To master a fine skill.

Ninety nights, ninety days,
Axing works hard day and night.
Axing is so diligent,
That he masters the craft in no time.

The wooden dragon he carves
Raises its head and swings its tail, playing with a pearl.
The phoenix he carves
Flies high in the sky.

Where there's a will, there's a way.
Two red candles shine brightly,
The master and the apprentice bid farewell at a dinner banquet,
And they toast each other three times.

The master pours the farewell wine,
And the appretice offers a cup of gratitude.
Each cup of wine tastes exceptionally sweet.
The bond between them will never be broken.

Bidding farewell to the master, he's about to leave.
Axing kneels before his master with reverence.
So many words to say, but he's unable to speak.
Tears flow like a spring.

"父母爱抚早失去，
你像父母般温暖。
先教我做正直人，
再教我手艺。

"给我凌空的羽翼，
给我翱翔的本领。
师徒虽别恩情重，
永世记在心。"

阿杏肩挑重担子，
跋山涉水出远门。
告别师父奔异乡，
离开众乡亲。

二、巧名传四方

晴天霹雳难预料，
忽然地震房屋倒。
阿杏日夜赶回家，
日夜救灾忙。

男女老少齐出力，
恢复家园修住房。
石头运来一堆堆，
木料一场场。

金场石头砌石脚，
三甸木料做梁柱。

"I lost my parents at a young age,
But you have been like a father to me.
You taught me to be an honest person,
And then you taught me your craft.

"You've given me wings to soar,
and the ability to fly high.
Though we are separated, our bond remains strong.
Your kindness I'll never forget."

With luggage on his shoulder,
Axing crossed mountains and rivers, traveling far.
Bidding farewell to his master,
He sets off for a new place.

II. Well-Known Craftsmanship

As unexpected as the thunder on a sunny day,
Houses suddenly collapse in an earthquake.
Axing hurried home day and night,
To help in the disaster around the clock.

Men, women, young and old work together,
To rebuild their homes and restore their lives.
Piles of stones are brought in,
And stacks of woods fill the yards.

Stones from the gold mine are used for the foundation,
Wood is used for beams and columns.

房屋修起一排排，
乡亲有住处。

过了寒冬花又香，
枯树回春绿叶飘。
风调雨顺庄稼好，
农民开颜笑。

风和日丽光景美，
柳荫花香衣食足。
歌声伴着欢笑声，
人说运气出。

但愿神仙来保佑，
金村重修本主庙。
公推阿杏当山神，
让他把墨画。

洱海之滨泥水匠，
粉刷绘画盖云南。
泥水巧匠请过来，
各自显神通。

白晃晃的墙壁上，
画一图图山水画，
画山青青翠欲滴，
画水淙淙响。

Houses are built row by row,
Providing homes for villagers.

After the harsh winter, flowers bloom again.
Withered trees come back to life again with green leaves.
With favorable weather, crops grow well,
And the farmers smile with joy.

The weather is fine, the scene is beautiful,
With willow shade and flower fragrance, clothes and food are sufficient.
Songs and laughter accompany each other,
People say good luck comes naturally.

May the gods bless us,
Rebuild the temple in the golden village.
They unanimously chose Axing as the mountain god,
And ask him to paint with ink.

Craftsmen by the shores of Erhai Lake
Known for their plastering and paiting across Yunnan.
Skilled craftsmen are invited over
To display their unique skills.

On the bright white walls,
Landscape paintings are created.
The mountains are painted green and vivid.
The rivers are dipicted as clear and flowing.

画出鸟儿扇翅飞，
画出花朵十里香。
众称洱海泥水匠，
技术实在巧。

能人里头有能人，
巧匠之中有巧匠。
美好名声巧木匠，
从此传四方。

三、天涯寻情人

一年一次杏花红，
一年一次梨花香。
不知红了多少次，
多少回芬芳。

报春雀来了又去，
紫燕去了又回来。
燕去雀回多少回，
记也记不清。

只记得呀巧木匠，
年纪已经二十几。
这么大的小伙子，
还没有情侣。

Birds in the painting flap their wings and soar.
Flowers in the painting spread a fragrance for miles around.
People praise the craftsmen from Erhai Lake.
Their skills are truely remarkable.

Among the skilled, there are the truly exceptional.
Among the craftsmen, there are the truly ingenious.
The reputation of the master carpenter,
Spreads far and wide from here.

III. Seeking for Romance

The apricot flowers blossom once a year.
The pear flowers spread their fragrance once a year.
I can't remember how many times they've turned red,
How many times they've been fragrant.

The spring sparrows come and go.
The purple swallows fly back and forth.
How many times have they migrated?
I can't recall.

I only remember the skilled carpenter,
Who's already in his twenties.
Such a young man,
Yet still without a sweetheart.

别人出门回家来，
甜言蜜语暖心间。
寂寞不过巧木匠，
单身对空影。

巧木匠呀想媳妇，
就像金鱼恋清泉。
无奈他家贫如洗，
手长袖口短。

跨过九十条江河，
翻过九十架高山。
一心寻找心上人，
脚杆快跑断。

南到邓川和浪穹，
北至丽江玉龙山，
西走兰坪和福贡，
东到永白城。

巧木匠呀就是穷，
穷人脚下路不平。
要想找到心中人，
难如上青天。

When others go out and come back home,
Sweet words warm their hearts.
But the skilled carpenter is all alone,
Single, with only his shadow for company.

The skilled carpenter longs for a wife,
Like a goldfish yearning for the clear spring water.
But his family is so poor.
He has the will but lacks the way.

He crosses ninety rivers,
And climbs ninety mountains.
Determined to find his beloved.
He nearly ran his legs off.

He travels south to Dengchuan and Langqiong,
North to Yulong Mountain in Lijiang,
West to Lanping and Fugong,
And east to Yongbai City.

Oh, poor carpenter!
For the poor, the road is never smooth.
To find his beloved,
It's as hard as climbing to the heavens.

四、鸳鸯梦

一个风雷交加夜，
巧木匠呀很疲倦。
迷迷糊糊入梦中，
观音母出现。

满头白发老婆婆，
金光面容慈悲心。
双手合掌到鼻尖，
口念《金刚经》。

“巧木匠呀巧木匠，
巧上加巧下功夫。
巧斗一架三弦琴，
巧绘鸳鸯图。”

巧木匠呀醒过来，
思考梦中的奥秘。
准是观音显神灵，
喜从天上来。

他去老君山找料，
找来馨香的檀木。
他又跑遍三甸箐，
找来秋木树。

IV. Dream of Romance

On a stormy night of wind and thunder,
The skilled carpenter is very tired.
He falls into a hazy sleep,
And Guanyin appears in his dream.

An old woman with gray hair,
Her face is radiant with golden light, full of compassion.
She clasps her hands together at her nose,
Reciting the *Diamond Sutra*.

"Oh Axing, oh Axing,
You are truely a master of your craft.
With your skill, you can create a three-stringed lute,
And paint a pair of mandrain ducks."

Axing wakes up,
Pondering the mistery of the dream.
It must be Guanyin showing her devine power,
Bringing him joy from the heaven.

He goes to Mount Laojun to find materials,
To search fragrant sandalwood.
He travels through the Sandianjing area,
And finds autumn wood trees.

不知跑了多少天，
所需原料备齐全。
精雕细刻琴龙头，
三弦斗成功。

五、白鸟会亲

精巧木匠斗三弦，
黄金龙头银丝线。
琴声幽幽感动人，
好像牵心绳。

鸟雀听到三弦声，
百鸟欢歌来聚会，
独有一只金翅鸟，
飞来龙头边。

嘴像银珠一样红，
尾毛豆叶般嫩绿。
翅膀一扇金闪闪，
腹毛白如棉。

巧木匠呀想捉鸟，
金翅鸟哟又飞掉。
三弦铮铮响起来，
鸟又飞回来。

After many days of searching,
He gathers all the necessary materials.
He intricately carves the dragon head,
And successfully complets the three-stringed lute.

V. The White Bird Couple

The skilled carpenter plays the three-stringed lute,
With a golden dragon head and silver threads.
Its haunting melody is deeply moving,
Like a thread that ties hearts together.

Birds and sparrows, hearing the sound,
Gather to sing in joy.
Only a golden-winged bird
Flies to rest by the dragon head.

Its beak is as red as silver beads.
Its tail feathers are as green as soybean leaves.
Its wings shimmer with a golden glown.
Its belly feathers are as white as cotton.

The skilled carpenter wants to catch the bird,
But the golden-winged bird flies away.
When the three-stringed lute rings out,
The bird flies back again.

琴声迷住金翅鸟，
好像蜜蜂钻花心。
清水白米享不尽，
木匠待它好。

巧木匠呀做木工，
金翅鸟哟唱起歌，
歌声美妙传情谊，
心里多快活。

可是木匠又思量，
不该关住金翅鸟。
要是它也有爹妈，
日子怎么熬？

“金翅鸟啊金翅鸟，
放你快快飞回家。
你爹你妈挂念你，
你也想爹妈。”

“我的阿爹和阿妈，
早去遥远的地方。
我和你啊一样命，
何处把身安？”

金翅鸟啊叫三声，
拍打三下金翅膀。
蓦然金光闪了闪，
变成个姑娘。

The golden-winged bird is attracted by the music,
Like a bee diving into the heart of a flower.
Providing clear water and food enough,
The carpenter treats it with kindness.

When the skilled carpenter works on his craft,
The golden-winged bird begins to sing.
Its beautiful melody conveys friendship and love,
Bringing joy to his heart.

But soon the carpenter ponders:
The golden-winged bird shouldn't be caged.
What if it has parents too?
How could they survive without it?

"Oh, little birdie, little birdie!
Fly home quickly!"
Your father and mother miss you.
And you must miss them too."

"My father and mother
Have long departed to a distant place.
I share the same fate with you.
Where can I find my place to stand?"

The golden-winged bird cries thrice,
And flapps its wings thrice.
In a sudden flash of gold,
A maiden appears.

姑娘彩霞般美丽，
像朵鲜艳的荷花。
眼儿星星一般亮，
眉毛似月牙。

氆氇领褂哑布衣，
金银耳环两边摆。
白银三须叮当响，
腰间飘花带。

人说凤凰最美啊，
怎能比得上姑娘。
就是漂亮的孔雀，
见她也躲藏。

姑娘名字叫梨花，
恰似紫燕来寻巢。
她要把深情厚谊，
献给巧木匠。

东山岭上有青藤，
青藤紧紧绕青松。
巧木匠配梨花女，
青藤绕青松。

The girl is as beautiful as colorful clouds,
Like a bright lotus in full bloom.
Her eyes are bright as stars.
Her eyebrows curve like crescent moons.

She wears a woolen-collared jacket and a coarse cloth gown,
With gold and silver earrings hanging on both sides.
Silver tassels jingle softly
And a floral belt sways around her waist.

They say phoenix is the most beautiful,
But how can it compare to this girl?
Even the most beautiful peacock,
Would hide in her presence.

Her name is Lihua.
Like a purple swallow seeking its nest,
She brings her deep affection
To the skilled carpenter.

On the eastern mountain ridge, a green vine
Clings tight to the green pine,
The carpenter with Lihua,
Together, like vine and pine.

六、相思

山花阵阵放清香，
漾江盈盈跃鱼虾。
谁料阳春落寒霜，
皇帝修宫房。

晴空霎时滚乌云，
人间无处不悲哀。
皇宫欢乐一夜晚，
百姓穷十年。

有钱的人派出钱，
有粮的人派出粮。
圣旨逼令巧木匠，
进京做木工。

好比鱼儿断了水，
好比绵羊被狼拖。
恩爱夫妻被拆散，
怎能有活路。

巧木匠呀被抓走，
梨花气碎了心肝，
她一粒饭也不咽，
一滴水不喝。

VI. Lovesickness

Mountain flowers bloom, releasing waves of fragrance.
The river brims with leaping fish and shrimp.
Who would have thought that frost would fall in spring?
And the emperor decrees build a palace.

The clear sky suddenly turns dark,
Bringing sorrow to every corner of the world.
One night of joy in the palace
Leaves the common fork in poverty for a decade.

The wealthy contribute money,
The well-staked offer their food.
By imperial decree, the skilled carpenter
Is compelled to work in the capital as craftman.

Like a fish without water,
A lamb in the wolf's mouth,
The loving couple is torn apart.
How can they go on living?

The skilled carpenter is taken away,
Leaving Lihua heartbroken.
She won't swallow a single grain of rice,
Nor drink a drop of water.

三次梨树枝枯残，
三次梨树长绿叶。
苦命人的辛酸泪，
恰似漾江水。

紫燕三次来孵儿，
紫燕三次回故乡。
梨花羡慕双飞燕，
相思巧木匠。

大雁三次来南方，
大雁三次回北方。
梨花想变成大雁，
万里去寻夫。

“多谢大雁行行好，
替我带封家书去，
告诉我的心上人，
妻我想念他。”

光阴闪闪像飞箭，
岁月滚滚似水流，
年复一年又一年，
不见木匠归。

梨花哭破了喉咙，
梨花哭肿了眼睛，
抬头喊天天不应，
钻地又无门。

The pear tree withers
And then greens three times over.
Bitter tears of the miserable
Flow like the river's endless stream.

The purple swallow thrice comes to hatch her young.
Thrice she returns to her homeland.
Lihua envies the swallows flying in pairs,
Longing for her beloved carpenter.

The wild geese thrice fly to the south and north,
Thrice they return to the north.
Lihua wishes she were a wild goose,
To fly a thousand of miles to find her husband.

"Kind wild geese, please do me a favor,
Carry this letter to my beloved,
And tell him
That his wife misses him so much."

Time flies!
Years roll like flowing water,
Year after year.
The carpenter still does not return.

Lihua cries until her voice is hoarse.
Her eyes swollen from weeping.
She looed up and calls to the heaven, but no answer.
She wishes to bury herself, but no way out.

七、抢婚

漾江水里藏着蛇，
自由鱼儿要受害。
坏人盘踞的地方，
香花也不鲜。

江东有个张有财，
满口毒牙满口甜，
喝够穷人的血液，
是个害人精。

他已娶了九房妻，
还想第十次结婚，
看见梨花容貌美，
口淌三尺涎。

他叫麻姑做媒婆，
去找梨花说姻缘。
花言巧语夸大话，
把梨花欺骗。

“张家金银堆如山，
你一辈子花不完。
绫罗绒丝锦绸缎，
够你穿百年。

VII. Marriage Robbing

Where a snake lurks in the river,
The fish are bound to be in peril.
Where the wicked dwell,
Even the sweetest flowers lose their fragrance.

There is a man named Zhang Youcai in Jiangdong,
With a mouth full of honeyed words and venomous teeth.
He thrives on the blood of the poor,
A veritable villain.

He has already married nine wives,
Yet he still yearns for a tenth.
At the sight of Lihua's beauty,
He drools yard long.

He asks Magu to be the matchmaker,
To approach Lihua and propose marriage.
With honeyed words and exaggerated tales,
The matchmaker deceives Lihua.

"The Zhang family has mountains of gold and silver,
Enough wealth to last a lifetime;
Silk, velvet, brocade, and satin,
Enough clothes for a hundred years.

"张家白米花眼睛，
张家井水会回甜。
南庄田来北庄地，
日子比蜜甜。

"一日三餐鱼和肉，
山珍海味吃不完。
若你愿意嫁给他，
终生有福享。

"再说你的巧木匠，
好比石头沉大海，
永远不会来相见，
快把心意转。"

蛤蟆想吃天鹅肉，
狗肚子里没香的。
梨花咬牙瞪白眼，
将麻姑撵开。

一只乌鸦飞过来，
歇在茅屋呱呱啼。
梨花预料要出事，
出门察风声。

恰巧乡邻来报信，
可恶有财要抢婚。
叫声梨花快快跑，
免省得受罪。

"The Zhang family has piles of rice.
Their well water tastes sweet.
With fields in the south and land in the north,
Life is sweeter than honey.

"There would be fish and meat for every meal,
With endless delicacies from land and sea.
If you are willing to marry him,
You will enjoy a lifetime of happiness.

"As for your skilled carpenter,
He is like a stone that has stuck into the deep sea.
He will never come back to you,
So be realistic."

Like a toad longing for the swan's flesh,
And dogs that only like stinky things,
Lihua clenches her teeth and glares,
And she drives Magu away.

A crow flies over,
Landing on a thatched roof and caws.
Lihua senses impending trouble,
So she stepps outside to check.

Suddenly a neighbor comes over,
Saying that Zhang plans to force her into marriage.
He shouts to Lihua, "Run quickly,"
To escape the suffering that awaits.

只见有财冲在前，
后头跟着一群人。
好像饿狼见绵羊，
三路扑过来。

天昏地暗日无光，
梨花要往哪儿逃？
四处都是张家人，
地上无生路。

八、夫妻相会

梨花飞跑到江边，
迎面又有人拦截。
面前只有一条路，
跳入漾江里。

每当太阳出东山，
漾江上空玉龙飞。
日月星辰来指引，
向京城飞去。

梨花虽死不瞑目，
天涯海角寻丈夫。
在耀眼的光彩中，
满足了愿望。

Zhang rushes over,
Followed by a crowd of people.
Like hungry wolves seeing a lamb,
They pounce from three directions.

The sky turns dark, and the sun disappears.
Where can Lihua run to escape?
The Zhang family's people are all around,
And there is no way out.

VIII. Husband and Wife's Reunion

Lihua runs to the riverbank,
But someone intercepts her.
There is only one way ahead,
And she jumps into the river.

Every time the sun rises over the eastern mountains,
A jade dragon soars above the river.
Guided by the sun, the moon, and the stars,
It flies towards the capital city.

Though Lihua dies with eyes unclosed,
Her spirit roams the ends of the earth to find her husband.
In a blaze of dazzling night,
Her wishes are finally fulfilled.

年年七月七傍晚，
天边出现朵云霞。
那是梨花巧木匠，
相会彩霞乡。

Every year on the evening of the Chinese Valentine's Day,
A beautifu cloud appears in the sky.
It's said that this is Lihua and her skilled carpenter,
Meeting in the land of rosy clouds.